The Rising Minister

A Sherlock Holmes Uncovered Tale

Steven Ehrman

D1713881

ISBN: **1497442133**
ISBN-13: **978-1497442139**

DEDICATION

To Spring, the season of new hope.

CONTENTS

WORKS BY THE SAME AUTHOR

The Sherlock Holmes Uncovered Tales
The Eccentric Painter
The Iron Dog
The Mad Judge
The Spider Web
The Lambs Lane Affair
The Rising Minister
Coming Soon – Robin Hood's Revenge

The Frank Randall Mysteries
The Referral Game
The Visible Suspect

The Zombie Civilization Saga
Zombie Civilization: Genesis
Zombie Civilization: Exodus
Coming Soon:
Zombie Civilization: Numbers

CHAPTER ONE

It was a pleasant day and I felt in quite good spirits as I crossed the threshold to my former rooms at 221B Baker Street. Although I had married some years before, I still managed to visit my good friend Sherlock Holmes when our combined schedules allowed.

Holmes gave me a friendly nod at my entrance and waved me to a seat. He was engaged in one of his favorite pastimes, which consisted of reading the criminal news and agony columns of London's many newspapers. At present, I perceived he was occupied by the *Daily Telegraph*. The sister publications to that paper lay in an unkempt heap by Holmes's chair. I lit a cigarette and waited for the great man to finish his task. In a matter of minutes he had consumed the last morsel to be had from the fourth estate and turned his attention towards me. I noticed his shrewd eye examining my person.

"I perceive that Mrs. Watson is out of town, Doctor," said he.

"That is true," said I, chuckling at the casual ease by which Holmes made his deductions, "but I must confess that I do not see how you could possibly know such a thing. Is my appearance so slovenly that you perceive the lack of a woman's touch?"

"Not at all, my friend. It is a clue only someone of close acquaintance might observe. In fact, I daresay that I alone am capable of this specific deduction."

"You intrigue me, Holmes," I said earnestly. "I insist you tell me of what you speak."

"It is a trivial matter to be sure, Watson, but when I see you wearing that particular tie I am certain that the good Mrs. Watson is not to be found in the city."

"I am afraid that I do not quite follow your reasoning, Holmes," I said slowly with downcast eyes.

"Oh, but I believe that you do, Doctor, though you would feign ignorance in order to shield my feelings," said Holmes with a twinkle. "I happen to know that your spouse detests that paisley tie you are wearing today."

"But, Holmes, this tie was given to me by you as a Christmas gift several years past."

"My very point, Doctor," replied Holmes. "The lady does not care for the tie, so you only wear it when she is out of town. You make a point of wearing it, during those circumstances, when you visit me as a demonstration of your appreciation."

I had tried to maintain a neutral expression on

my face as Holmes had described Mary's dislike of Holmes's choice of neckwear, but he was correct as always. My dear wife simply hated the tie in question. As Holmes finished, I broke into a smile and raised my hands in surrender.

"I give up, Holmes," said I. "It is true that the tie languishes low in Mary's esteem, but please believe that the attitude pertains only to the gift and not to the bearer of the gift."

"I am well aware of that, Doctor, and I return her cordiality, even if her entrance into your life signaled the end of our sharing of these diggings."

"It was love, and not my own free will, Holmes, that drove the decision."

"As one unafflicted with that particular emotion, I will take your word for it, Watson."

"In any event, Holmes, you are correct and Mary is tending to a sick aunt in Sussex," said I.

"I say, Watson, is it my imagination or is Mrs. Watson away a great deal of the time?"

"You speak for me, old friend, but she cannot refuse her family when they are in need. Was my choice of tie the only deduction you have gleaned from your observations?"

"Not quite," said he. "Another deduction, Watson, is that you are dressed quite nattily, differing opinions about your tie notwithstanding. Do you have an engagement besides this visit?"

"I have been invited to a luncheon at the home of Clive Brown."

"The junior minister?" asked Holmes with a raised eyebrow.

"The very one," said I.

"He was a brother physician at one time, or am I mistaken?

"That he was, Holmes," I said.

Clive Brown was an old friend of mine who had chucked medicine for a life in government. It had seemed an odd decision to me at the time, but Clive, and his wife, seemed satisfied with the career change.

"Mycroft says that Brown is a rising man and he would know, of course," said Holmes.

"I had no idea that they were acquainted?"

"They aren't," replied Holmes, "but men being groomed for high positions are watched closely. I would not be surprised to see him in the Cabinet one day."

"That would be a grand thing for him," I mused. "Of course, I will always remember him as the young scamp and rascal with the ladies. How his dear wife Victoria put up with him in their early years is beyond me."

My memories went back to my own younger days. I felt middle age creeping up on me and the youthful days seemed far away. I allowed myself to bask in their memory for a bit. After some minutes, the voice of Sherlock Holmes broke my reverie.

"Do you see much of the junior minister these days?" asked Holmes.

"I fear not. Our paths do not cross nearly as much as when he still practiced medicine. However, we try and renew our friendship several times a year. This luncheon is being given to honor his American relatives. I have never met them, but I understand that they are a distant male cousin and his wife. It is said that the cousin is a millionaire, but then all Americans seem to be millionaires these days."

"I would imagine as many fortunes are lost as are won, Watson," observed Holmes.

I was ruminating over that idea when he continued.

"Then I take it that this is to be a social

gathering and not an intimate affair."

"That is so, though I am not privy to the guest list. I assume that, besides the American relatives, there will be any number of ministers or government officials in attendance, as that is the host's social circle these days."

"And yet you, an old friend, are invited as well."

"I hold my friends, old and new, in high regard and I am glad my host does also," I said with a short laugh. "It will be a pleasant diversion, at any rate."

Holmes agreed and we spent the next several hours in conversation. When he was in an expansive mood, as it seemed he was today, Holmes could be a very stimulating companion. He held forth over the rest of my visit on a wide range of topics and I was surprised when I realized that it was time for me to take my leave of the man.

Holmes bade me farewell and extracted a promise that I return for another visit before my dear Mary returned. I happily assented and left.

The day was quite fair, if very warm, and I considered walking to my appointment, but I had tarried too long with Holmes and I hailed a hansom instead. I gave the driver the address and we set off at a brisk pace through the streets of the grand old city. In what seemed like little time, we arrived at the Brown residence. I stepped out, paid the driver, and began to stroll up the short walk to the home. It was a stately house that frankly appeared to be beyond Clive's means, but I remembered that he received an inheritance from an uncle some years back. That undoubtedly explained the grand living quarters.

I knocked at the front entrance and was greeted by a grave and proper servant. I remembered him as the long-time butler of the Brown household, Perkins.

"Well, Perkins, it is good to see you," I said in greeting.

"I assure you, sir, that the pleasure is mine," said he in a suave tone.

"Dear me," I said as I glanced around what I could see of the house. "Am I the first to arrive?"

"You are indeed, sir."

"Is your master about?" I asked.

"The master was called away, sir, but he tasked me with assuring all his guests that he would make a timely return."

"What of Mrs. Brown then?"

"She is in the dining room at present, sir,"

intoned Perkins.

"Then perhaps I can pay my respects to her," I suggested.

"Of course, sir. Walk this way please."

I followed the butler down a long hallway. Presently we came to a large set of double doors. He opened them and the dining room hove into view. Perkins announced me and I entered. I immediately saw that Victoria Brown was with two servants and was instructing them in the setting of the table.

"Why, Doctor," she cried. "How good of you to come today."

"I thank you for inviting me, but I fear I am early and I am upsetting your arrangements."

"Not at all, Doctor," she replied.

"If there is nothing else, madam," said Perkins.

"Of course, please see to your duties."

"Thank you, madam," he said and withdrew with a stiff bow.

Left alone with the lady and the other servants, I scanned the scene. The table was set for twelve and was nearly complete. I observed the two servants. One was a boy of some fourteen years and quite thin, with a shock of red hair and a pleasant, eager face. The other was a girl of roughly sixteen years. She was blonde and rather stout with a distinctly German appearance. They were busily setting out cutlery and plates. I had just turned my attention back to the lady of the house when I heard a loud crash and breaking of glass. As I turned I saw the boy shamefaced and looking at his mistress with something approaching dread.

"Why, John, how clumsy you are," said Victoria Brown coldly.

"I am so very sorry, Mrs. Brown. It was an accident. The plate slipped from my hand, just like it had been greased, it did."

The boy began his speech in the squeaky tone of an adolescent boy, but halfway through his voice broke and a hesitant baritone took its place. The servant girl, Judith, laughed out loud and was rewarded with a withering look from the lady.

"That will be quite enough of that, Judith," snapped Victoria Brown.

"Yes, mum," said the girl, properly chastened.

"Now, John, get that cleaned up and, Judith, run to the kitchen and get another setting," she said. "I tell you, Doctor," turning back to me, "sometimes I wonder if servants are worth all the trouble they bring with them. Judith is hopeless, though she has been here for years. John is even worse and he comes from the servant class. His mother was in service here twenty years ago. She left, without notice I might add, and took up a trade as a seamstress in Chelmsford. When she died we took in her son. But it is hard to find those even willing to go into service these days, so there is something in that anyway. I blame the government. Oh, Doctor, I hope I am not boring you with my domestic troubles."

I smiled a reply and watched as the girl exited quickly by a door at the far end of the room. The young lad swept the shards of glass into a rubbish bin and followed her out the same door. The girl was gone for only a minute and when she returned she had a new plate for the table. She put it down in its proper spot, taking the place of the broken one, and looked to her mistress.

"Cook says she needs to speak with you, mum," she said with a wooden expression.

"Very well, Judith. Tell her I will be along."

The girl curtsied and left again.

"What now?" asked the lady grimly.

CHAPTER TWO

As if in answer to her question, a young lad strode into the room. I recognized him at once as my friend's son, Gerald. He was thirteen as I recalled, and painfully thin, as his father had been in his youth. He stopped when he saw us and looked around in confusion.

"What is it, Gerald?" asked his mother.

"I thought Father was in here," said the boy.

"Well, he's not, as you can plainly see," she said.

"Mother, it was only that-" he began, before his mother cut him off.

"I am not interested in your train of thought just now, Gerald," Victoria Brown said. "Go and find your sister and tell her I need her."

The young lad scurried from the room under the glare of his mother. There was a slight undercurrent of tension, and I was about to excuse myself from the dining room when I heard the booming voice of my friend, Clive Brown.

"Victoria! Where are you?" he said.

"I am in the dining room, which you would know if you gave it half a thought before bellowing," she replied acidly.

In just a few moments my old friend came into the room with the bashful grin of a truant schoolboy. He seemed startled yet pleased when he saw me there ahead of him.

"Why, Watson, how happy I am to find you here," said he. "We see so little of each other these days."

"I seem to be seeing a bit more of you these days, my friend," I said eyeing his bulging middle. My once slender friend was growing quite stout in his middle years.

"Blame it on domestic bliss, Watson," he said, patting his stomach. "It will happen to you too."

I shared a laugh with him and we excused ourselves from the room. He led me back down the hallway.

"What say you to a smoke before we dine, Watson?" he asked.

I was agreeable, and my host led me toward the library of the house. Before we arrived there, Clive was accosted by a red-haired whirlwind. A young girl had come running down the hall and had thrown herself into his arms.

"Oh, Father," she exclaimed. "Miss Hopkins has been just dreadful to me today."

"Your governess is paid to be dreadful to you, my dear," returned her father with a laugh. "Besides, I believe by dreadful, you mean she is making you study your books."

"But I want to go to the luncheon with you and Mother," pouted the beautiful little girl.

"The luncheon is only for the adults, as you well know. Now run along. Your father has guests to attend to."

He put the girl back down and she raced out of sight around a corner. Clive took me by the arm and led me into the library with a sigh. The library was a spacious room with two leather sofas and with three times as many chairs. My host and I each settled into a chair. I lit a cigarette and Clive did likewise.

"She is the apple of my eye, Watson, but we have spoiled her terribly," he said, blowing out a cloud of smoke.

"Oh, hardly that, I think, Doctor," I said with a smile.

"I am not a physician any longer, old boy."

"Minister then."

"A humble junior minister, I assure you," he replied.

"I am told by a reliable authority that you are being measured for higher office."

"What reliable authority?" he asked, leaning forward in eagerness.

Holmes had not sworn me to any secrecy, so I related the conversation he and I had had. A broad smile crossed Clive's face as he listened.

"I have heard the same tale, but I did not dare believe it true," he said. "This could be the culmination of all that I have worked for, Watson."

The conversation carried on for some minutes on the subject of a possible cabinet post for my friend, when the door to the library was thrown open. A tall man of medium build walked in very quickly. He was wearing a finely-tailored suit and had a bristling mustache.

"Clive, I caught another of your staff nosing

through my things this morning," he said, wagging a finger in Clive's face. His accent immediately betrayed him as Clive Brown's American cousin. "Yesterday it was the little fat girl and today I saw your young page-boy coming out of my room. I will not stand for it, I say."

"John, please calm yourself," said my host. "The servants have to enter your room to bring wood for the fireplace, to return laundry, and any number of other tasks. One would think that you had never had a servant."

"We have them, of course, but they know their place in America."

"I am certain they do," said Clive wryly. "However, I am forgetting my manners. John Thompson, allow me to introduce you to Dr. John Watson. This is my dear wife's cousin."

"And your cousin as well, Clive," said the man earnestly. "Wouldn't you like a rich cousin? Your Queen may someday knight you, but you cannot live on titles."

"I am doing just fine, I assure you," said Clive motioning at the walls around him. It was obvious to me that his wife's relation was irritating him, but the American seemed blithely ignorant of the animus.

"Oh yes, this is nice enough, I suppose, but I could fit the entire house in one wing of mine."

I decided to jump in and change the subject.

"Where in America do you reside, Mr. Thompson?" I asked.

"We hail from Montana, Doctor," he said with gusto. "I made my fortune in timber. If there is one thing that Montana has that the world needs, it's timber. Clive could do worse than to throw in with me."

John Thompson laughed at his joke, but neither Clive nor I did. I smiled politely, but Clive made no effort whatsoever.

"Well, gentlemen, I must find my wife before the other guests arrive," said the American. "I look forward to more conversation with you, Doctor."

With that statement the man left as quickly as he had arrived. Clive stubbed his cigarette out angrily and threw it in the unlit fireplace.

"The man is a bloody irritant," said he.

"Do you suppose he really is a millionaire?" I asked.

"He says he is many times over. Acts damn superior about it," muttered my friend.

Just then Perkins glided into the room.

"Your other guests are arriving, sir," he said.

"Thank you, Perkins," said Clive.

"Once more into the breach, Doctor," said my friend with a grin.

I arose, and Clive and I left the library.

The new guests were a mix of government officials and friends of the hosting couple. The meal was a hearty repast of roast beef and ham. Generous portions of vegetables were included along with a very passable pudding and pie.

I found myself seated next to the wife of John Thompson. She was a languid, dreamy sort of woman. Her name was Betty, which I was certain was not her given name, but rather a derivative of the more elegant, Elizabeth. Brown's American female cousin was much less formal than a comparable Englishwoman and she made free with my first name, to my slight distaste.

John Thompson dominated the conversation at every turn. He seemed to consider himself an expert on nearly every topic. My friend Clive was clearly made uncomfortable by his boorish behavior, but the American seemed immune to any hints that his opinion was not desired from all in attendance. I noticed Clive shooting an angry look at his wife, which she gave back in turn.

At the completion of the meal, the men of the group followed Clive's suggestion that we retire to the library. This was agreed to by acclamation and within minutes I had reclaimed my chair from my previous visit. John Thompson left after finishing one pipe, pleading that he needed to see to his wife. His absence caused a thaw in the atmosphere and I found myself in a convivial conversation with a junior minister who had recently returned to England after a trade mission to India.

I enjoyed myself so much that I completely lost track of time and was astonished when I realized that I had to take my leave. Clive was nowhere to be seen, so I excused myself from the library and went in search of him, and Victoria, to pay my respects to my hosts before I left.

Once in the hallway I hesitated, wondering if Clive had returned to the dining room. I espied Perkins coming from that direction and hailed him.

"I say, Perkins, where can I find your master?"

"I believe that he is in the study, sir," intoned the butler. "Shall I show you the way?"

"That will not be necessary. I know the way."

"Very good, sir. If you will excuse me."

The butler went about his business and I set off.

The study was on the other end of the home and I whistled happily on the way. I nearly had my hand on the doorknob when I heard angry voices from within.

"I am heartily sick of this conversation," declared a voice I knew to be Clive Brown's. "They are your family, not mine."

"You do not want to begin with me in that vein, Clive," returned the voice of Victoria Brown.

The voices lowered somewhat so that the words became indistinct. I became aware of my status as an eavesdropper, however inadvertently, and knocked loudly at the door to announce my presence.

It was opened abruptly and Victoria Brown rushed by me without a word. Her face was flushed. Clive Brown was in the middle of the room with his hands thrust deep into his pockets. I felt extremely awkward and knew not just what to do. Clive, however, recovered his *savoir-faire* very quickly. He strode up to me and clapped me on the shoulder.

"Victoria is a bit nervy today," said he. "Organizing together our little gathering here has put her a little out of sorts."

"Of course," I replied, "it is the most natural thing in the world, but I fear I must take my leave."

"So soon?"

"Yes. I have enjoyed myself immensely and I thank you for having me, but the afternoon has completely run away and I must go."

After several more attempts to persuade me to change my mind, Clive walked me to the front entrance. Perkins appeared from nowhere with my hat and cane and I was off.

I walked some blocks before I hailed a hansom. Giving the driver my address, I reflected upon my afternoon. I did not envy my old friend in his social obligations. Relatives, even wealthy ones, are difficult guests in the best of circumstances.

Once home, I took up some correspondence that I had been neglecting. I wrote Mary of my day with the Browns, while diplomatically avoiding anything that could be termed gossip. I told her of the information that Holmes had relayed about the possible upswing in Clive's governmental career.

As the hour grew late, I equivocated upon whether or not to retire for the evening. As my quarters were temporarily of a bachelor nature, I decided that I would read and smoke a bit as I was not tired although I had had a full day.

I filled a pipe and pulled a copy of *Great*

Expectations from a bookshelf. I sat down and began reading. I soon lost myself in the prose of Dickens. Pip was a favorite character of mine and as a boy I had imagined myself as an orphan adrift in the world. My eyelids grew heavy, but I fought the impulse to sleep and tried to continue reading. I eventually fell asleep in my chair and did not awaken again until morning.

CHAPTER THREE

When I woke up, I felt a bit stiff from my night sleeping upright. I imagined that Mary would scold me if she found out that I had spurned my bed for such Spartan accommodations. She would surely lecture me on falling back into my bachelor days so soon after she had left, were she to find out. I knew I could count on discretion from the small staff and I determined she would not hear the tale from my lips either.

I had a quick breakfast and decided to once again visit Holmes on Baker Street. Arriving at my destination, I was shown up quickly by the page-boy and was ushered in. Holmes had also finished breakfast and was lounging in his dressing gown smoking a pipe. He greeted me and motioned towards a pile of shag tobacco. I deferred and lit a cigarette. Once I was seated, Holmes tapped out his bowl and turned to me.

"It is not often these days that you manage two visits in as many days, Doctor," said he with a twinkle.

I was about to reply when there was a fierce pounding on the downstairs door. The knocking soon ceased and was replaced by a clattering on the stairs. The door to the room was thrown open and Inspector Lestrade of Scotland Yard burst in.

"So, Doctor," he began, "instead of coming to the authorities I find you here instead. Or were you in on this from the beginning, Mr. Holmes?"

I looked at Holmes in bewilderment, but the taciturn detective gave no hint of his emotions and remained serene.

"Please, Inspector, you have us at a complete disadvantage," said he. "Pray be seated and tell us of the purpose of this unexpected visit."

"Unexpected, is it?" asked Lestrade with skepticism. "And I will sit when I have some answers. Dr. Watson, for what purpose did you visit the home of Mr. Clive Brown yesterday?"

"Why, to attend a luncheon, of course," I replied with some heat, as I chafed under Lestrade's tone. "Mr. Brown would tell you the same if you asked him."

"I will ask him, Doctor. Now, Mr. Holmes," he said turning his attention to my friend. "Did you send the doctor on an errand or as part of a case?"

"I did not, Inspector."

"Did you know he was going?"

"I did. In fact, he left from these rooms and went directly to the luncheon."

"Ah ha! So you admit you knew he was going."

"I do not admit it, I state it. Now really, this is growing tiresome, even for you, Lestrade. What has happened at the Brown home for you to come here in such a state? Has something happened to Mr. Brown?"

"No, Mr. Holmes," the Inspector replied, "but murder has been done."

"Who?" I asked, on the edge of my seat.

"A young servant by the name of John Carpenter has been poisoned," said Lestrade. "Apparently the remains of yesterday's lunch were set aside in the pantry for the servants' dinner. They were to have the leftover roast beef. The ham was to be saved for the breakfast this morning; however, late last night the boy became violently ill after eating some of the ham and died within a half hour without speaking."

"How awful," I said.

"Awful indeed, Doctor," said the Inspector.

Lestrade finally decided to seat himself and he plopped into a chair next to mine. He ran his fingers through his hair in frustration.

"When I was notified of this crime and was told that the Doctor had been in attendance the previous day, I naturally assumed that you were behind it, Mr. Holmes."

"But why did it come to your attention at all, Inspector?" asked Holmes.

"Why not?" said Lestrade, suddenly wary.

"Come now, Inspector," said Holmes. "You are an experienced investigator and considered one of the top men at the Yard. Surely the death of a servant boy does not rise to your level."

"It is not the individual, but the place that calls for my attention," replied Lestrade.

"Because the death occurred in the home of Mr. Clive Brown, I assume."

"Yes, Mr. Holmes. He is a rising man and the circumstances of the poisoning seem to indicate that he was the actual target of this crime."

"I see," said Holmes. "Let me see if I understand your thinking. As the ham was served at lunch and no one there became ill, you deduce that the poison was introduced later."

"Of course, sir. Is there any other explanation?"

"Not with the information we have now. The ham was to be saved for the breakfast of the household the next day so it would seem that any one, or all of them could have been the intended target. Somehow the boy eats a portion of the ham first and dies. Is that a close outline of your thinking?"

"It is, but I have not yet been on the scene myself. When the report came to me and I saw the good doctor's name as a guest I came straight here."

"I see."

"Inspector," I began, "I can assure you that Clive Brown is simply an old friend and former professional colleague. I went at his invitation and had no ulterior motive."

"Very well, Doctor. I do not question your honesty," he said with a grim expression. "Can you give me an account of what occurred yesterday at the Brown residence? It may have a bearing on the crime, and you are an impartial observer."

"Yes, Watson," said Holmes. "Please try to recall all conversations as closely as you can. Anything you heard or observed may be important."

I spent the next half hour reviewing and repeating all I had seen and heard during the previous day. Lestrade made some notes, but Holmes wrote down nothing and asked few questions. At the end of my recitation Lestrade put away his notebook and rose as if to leave.

"I must be off then," he said. "The scene grows cold and I have a murderer to apprehend."

Holmes arose as well.

"Half a moment, Inspector," said he. "Allow me to change and we will join you."

"That is good news, sir," said Lestrade, visibly brightening. "After my entrance, I did not hope that you would lend a hand."

"Put it from your mind, Lestrade," said Holmes airily. "The game is afoot."

In less than five minutes we were being jolted down the cobbled streets of London. Holmes asked no more questions about the crime and Lestrade said little as well. For myself, I was simply glad that my friend Clive had not been injured, though, of course, I was saddened by the loss of life in one so young. After being deposited in front of the Brown home, we made our way through a throng of idlers that had gathered. Lestrade nodded to several uniformed officers. As he was obviously recognized, no one hindered our advancement. Once inside, Lestrade called out to a man in plain clothes talking with the butler, Perkins.

"Sharp," said Lestrade, "I would have a word with you."

"Yes, sir," said the man, scurrying to Lestrade's side.

Introductions were quickly made. Inspector Sharp was a young, clean-shaven man with an eager, alert face. When the name of Sherlock Holmes was spoken, I saw a look of respect from the man.

"I have heard of you, of course, Mr. Holmes," he said.

"Enough of that," snapped Lestrade. "I need to have a report from you, Sharp. Where can we speak in private?"

"The library is empty, sir," said a chastened Sharp.

"Very good. Lead the way."

Once in the library, Lestrade took control.

"Now, I have the bare facts, Sharp, but I want an update on the investigation," he said. "This case has drawn the interest of higher-ups."

"Why is that, sir?" asked the young Inspector.

"That is none of your business, Sharp," returned

Lestrade.

"Sir, surely any reason to think this case more than it appears is germane to the investigation."

Lestrade paused, as if considering the words of the younger man.

"Very well," he said finally. "Mr. Clive Brown is a man who is being groomed for a higher position in the Ministry. If he was the intended target of this crime, it could be a very bad business."

"A political crime, sir?" asked Sharp.

"Let us say that all avenues are to be investigated."

"Of course, sir."

"Having said that, let us not leap to conclusions," lectured Lestrade.

Before Lestrade could say more, the door opened and a heavyset, older man walked in. He carried a doctor's bag in one hand and a cane in the other.

"Ah, Lestrade, just the man I was looking for," said he.

"Dr. Martin," returned the Inspector. "What news do you have?"

"Well, the boy died of arsenic poisoning. There is no doubt of that."

"We already knew that," said Lestrade in an irritated manner.

"That was the surmise, but I am making it official," said the doctor, with no trace that he had noted Lestrade's irritation. "From all indications the lad ingested the poison some time after ten o'clock last evening. His death was relatively quick, but quite ugly, I assure you."

"Sharp, I understand the cook was with the boy at his death," said Lestrade.

"That is so, sir," said the man as he examined a notebook. "The cook, one Emma Barton, states that she was roused from her bed by the boy's cries. She estimates the time as two o'clock in the morning. By the time she reached his side he was past hope. She could make no sense of his words and the boy died before a doctor could be sent for."

"It would have made no difference," intoned Dr. Martin.

"And we have determined that the ham was poisoned? That is certain?"

"Yes, Inspector," replied Sharp. "The ham was

set aside for the morning meal. The servants did not eat it with their dinner. As no one became sick at the luncheon yesterday, it follows that the ham was poisoned later."

"Have you found the source of the arsenic?"

"That is no secret, sir. The house keeps a bit as rat poison. It is kept in a storage room off the kitchen. This is not uncommon."

"Dr. Martin," said Holmes quietly, "have you determined that the arsenic kept as rat poison is the same arsenic that killed the boy?"

The doctor looked to Lestrade.

"Inspector, who is this man?"

"This is Mr. Sherlock Holmes and he is aiding my investigation," said Lestrade. "Answer his question, please."

"Sherlock Holmes! Why, this business must be deeper than it seems," said the doctor, as he shot a glance at Lestrade. The Inspector merely shrugged and the doctor continued. "Well, of course, it is impossible to tell if the arsenic kept in the household is the same arsenic that killed the boy, but it seems likely."

"Do you doubt it, Mr. Holmes?" asked Lestrade.

"No, but I wonder how it is that the arsenic was discovered so quickly in the ham. The poison may have been introduced from a myriad of sources. How is that the focus came so quickly on the ham?"

"That is answered easily enough, sir," said Sharp. "The cook reported that there was a plate of it by the boy's bed. It was only natural that suspicion was focused immediately upon the ham."

"Was all the ham poisoned or just the plate by the boy's bedside?"

"We appreciated that point, sir," replied Sharp. "The ham in the larder was poisoned as well."

If Holmes was disappointed by that statement, he did not show it.

"Do you suggest a course of action, Mr. Holmes?" asked Lestrade.

"I would suggest two things, Inspector. Firstly, I would like to speak with the cook and secondly, the house should be thoroughly searched."

Steven Ehrman

CHAPTER FOUR

"**S**earched?" repeated Lestrade. "Searched for what?"

"Why, anything incriminating," replied Holmes blandly.

"That is hardly an answer, Mr. Holmes," said Lestrade.

"All I can add, Inspector, is that the men should pay particular attention to everyone's personal possessions. I think we will find something of interest along those lines."

Lestrade did not like the explanation, but he issued the proper instructions and had the cook brought to the library. Sharp left in order to supervise the search. After a brief word in private with Lestrade, Dr. Martin departed as well. He promised a report the next day for the Inspector.

The cook was escorted into the room by a sergeant. Emma Barton was an older, gaunt lady of some sixty years with grey hair in a severe bun. Lestrade asked her to be seated, but she declined and remained standing with a stiff, ramrod-straight carriage.

"Now, Miss Barton, how is it that you came to minister to the boy last night?" asked Lestrade.

"One of the girls heard him moaning and she naturally came to me."

"Which girl?" asked Holmes.

"Judith," replied the cook. "Her room was near to the boy and he woke her."

"How did the boy come to eat the ham, Miss Barton?" asked Lestrade.

"I cannot tell you, sir," said the cook, shaking her head. "It was to be set out with breakfast this morning and everyone knew it. He was very wicked to nip some for himself."

"And he said nothing to you while you were with him, is that correct?"

"Indeed not, Inspector. He was retching the whole time. He spoke not a word."

"Was a doctor sent for?"

"It all happened too fast, you see," said Miss Barton. Her eyes welled with tears at the memory. "I tried to give him a purgative. I thought he had just eaten something that had disagreed with him."

Holmes pounced. "So you thought right away that it was something he had eaten."

"Of course, sir."

"Then why," began Holmes in a brisk voice, "did you not worry about yourself or other members of the staff?"

"Well...it was just...just that the ham was on the nightstand," the lady stammered. "What else was I to think?"

"Nothing at all," said Holmes. "It turned out that you were quite right.

"You have been here a long time I take it."

"That is so, sir. Almost eighteen years in service to Mr. And Mrs. Brown. Why, I knew the boy's mother when she was in service here."

"Ah yes, the boy. Tell me, how do you think the lad came to take the ham?"

"I cannot say, sir. It is true that young servants these days all steal. Not like the old days, I can tell you that."

Steven Ehrman

"Did the lad like ham?"

"Who doesn't like ham, sir?"

"Allow me to state it another way. Did he have a special preference for ham?"

"He was greedy about food. I will say that."

"Perhaps he was hungry," said Holmes innocently. "I understand that the boy was quite thin. Underfed I should say."

"That is not true, sir," said the cook with a distressed tone. "The master and mistress make certain all of the staff are well-fed. And I would never let a child go hungry. No one wants in this house."

"But he was so thin," protested Holmes.

"That proves nothing. Judith is quite plump, thank you very much. Besides, that is simply how some boys are. They eat and eat and yet never gain weight. It is only when they become middle-aged that that it begins to show."

The gaunt cook looked directly at me as she finished her statement and I self-consciously pulled in my stomach.

"Is there anything else?" asked the woman.

"I think not," said Lestrade. "You may go."

The cook departed with a quiet dignity.

"Do you suspect her of some involvement in the boy's death?" asked Lestrade when she was gone.

"No, Inspector, I do not," said Holmes.

"Then why did you press her so hard on the cause of the boy's death?"

"It was only that I wished to hear from her own lips just how obvious it was that the ham was the culprit," said Holmes.

"But the ham was the cause, so what difference could it make?" asked the Inspector.

"Perhaps none, I admit," said Holmes in a faraway voice.

Before Lestrade could essay another question, Mr. John Thompson stormed into the room.

"Which of you is Inspector Lestrade?" he asked angrily.

He recognized me at once, and turned his attention to Holmes and Lestrade.

"I am Lestrade," said the Inspector. "By your accent, I take it that you are the American cousin, Mr.

Thompson."

"That is so, Inspector, and I demand to know by what right you propose to search my rooms."

"Mr. Thompson," said Lestrade patiently, "there has been a murder committed in this house. All avenues of investigation must be followed."

"Then, you dare to accuse me? It is ludicrous. I am a man of some influence, Inspector. You do not want to fall afoul of me. I will speak to the consulate."

"That is your prerogative, sir," said Lestrade. "The search, however, will go on."

"If that is your stance, my wife and I shall leave for a hotel."

"Not until the search is over," said Lestrade firmly.

The man could see at once that there was no use in arguing with the Inspector. He turned his attention to Holmes. He appraised him with shrewd eyes.

"I understand you are some sort of unofficial detective. You are Mr. Holmes. An English Pinkerton, is that it?"

"Nothing so ambitious, I assure you, Mr.

Thompson," replied Holmes with a smile. "Did you ever talk with the deceased boy?"

"Certainly not. Why should I?"

"I understand you have been here over a week. In that entire time you never exchanged a single word with the boy?"

"I have no time to shoot the breeze with servants, Mr. Holmes," declared the man.

I was bewildered by the idea of shooting breezes, but Holmes evidently was more familiar with American idioms than I as he seemed to understand perfectly.

"Watson tells me that you made your fortune in timber," said Holmes. "There must be a great need for timber in a growing country such as the United States."

"You are right there, sir," said the man with obvious earnestness. "The country is on the move. It's no wonder we pulled away from this rainy island. Let me tell you of my plans."

Thompson went on in this vein for some time. Holmes seemed eager to listen and let the man drone along without interruption. We were finally saved when his wife glided into the room.

Oh, there you are, John," she said dreamily.

"Please come back to the dining room. Clive is pacing back and forth and Victoria talks of nothing but her children. It is dreadfully boring."

Introductions were made all around. If Mrs. Thompson recalled me from yesterday, it was not apparent. Soon husband and wife left together.

"That is a thoroughly vacuous woman," said Lestrade, after the pair had exited the room.

"Is that how she struck you, Inspector?" asked Holmes.

"What else? But that is neither here nor there," said the Inspector. "And what was that feigned interest in Mr. Thompson's opinions?"

"Feigned?" asked Holmes innocently.

"Yes, feigned, Mr. Holmes. I know you do not consider me a detective on par with yourself, but give me enough credit to spot when you are setting one of your traps."

"It was not precisely a trap, Inspector," said Holmes with a slight smile. "My conversation with Mr. Thompson served two purposes. The man presents himself as a millionaire American businessman, but is it true?"

"Do you doubt him, Holmes?" I asked.

"No, Doctor, but if he is other than he says it could mean that he has something to hide. Perhaps even something to kill to protect."

"But wouldn't Mrs. Brown know if her own cousin was misrepresenting himself?" I asked.

"Really, Doctor," scoffed Holmes. "They are separated by an ocean. An unscrupulous man could take advantage of that, but that is beside the point. My conversation with the man has convinced me he is what he appears."

"Very well, Mr. Holmes," said Lestrade. "That covers your first reason. What of your second reason for this discussion with Thompson?"

"Ah, that," said Holmes. "That was simply to keep him occupied during the search and distract him from what such a search might find."

"So you still think he might be hiding something even after establishing his *bona fides* to your satisfaction," said I. "What makes you so certain of that?"

"You related to me the conversation that Mr. Thompson had with Mr. Brown in which he was angry at the staff for being in his room. The anger, it seems to me, is quite out of proportion to the annoyance. The natural conclusion is the man is hiding something."

"Something that you believe to have a bearing on the case," said the Inspector.

"Perhaps. It is difficult to predict."

"I see," said Lestrade. "Shall we have the Browns in next?"

"I would advise against that, Inspector," said Holmes. "I would save them until last."

"Who then?" Lestrade asked.

"I understand there is a governess in residence. I would like to interview her."

Lestrade agreed and gave the orders. Within minutes a tall, gaunt lady of late middle age appeared in the room. She had on a modest grey skirt and blouse with her graying hair in a bun. It occurred to me that she and the cook could be taken for sisters. Lestrade invited her to sit and she did so, taking a seat on a sofa.

"You are Miss Hopkins," stated Lestrade.

"I am, sir," said the lady primly.

"How long have you been the governess for the Browns?"

"Two years next month," came the prompt reply.

"Have you seen anything that might shed light on this tragedy?"

"Heavens no, sir."

The very idea of being associated with any type of scandal seemed mortifying to the woman.

"Did you yourself know the dead boy?"

"Why, of course, I knew his name, but I do not believe I ever had a conversation with him."

"What about the children?" asked Holmes.

"What about them, sir?"

"Did they have contact with the dead boy?"

"Oh, I see what you mean now," she said. "Mrs. Brown does not permit the staff and the family to socialize, sir."

"Of course, but Gerald Brown is only a bit younger than the dead boy. They must have played together."

"Not to my knowledge, sir."

"That would seem quite unlikely," insisted Holmes.

"I have told you what I know," she said coldly.

Holmes lapsed into silence. Lestrade took that as evidence that Holmes was finished with the governess.

"That will be all for now, Miss Hopkins," he said. "Except I would like to know your previous employer."

"That would be Colonel Marston. He returned to India two years ago. He wrote me a wonderful letter of recommendation before he left. I can show it to you if you like."

Lestrade told her that would not be necessary at the present and escorted her to the door. As the door opened, I heard the voice of Gerald Brown arguing with his sister down the hall and out of sight.

"Not much new information there, Mr. Holmes," said Lestrade.

"No," admitted Holmes, "but it was necessary."

"Why?" demanded the Inspector.

Holmes did not reply and Lestrade shot me a frustrated look. I merely shrugged. I had learned through weary repetition that Sherlock Holmes doled out information at his own pace and could not be stampeded into action. Inspector Sharp chose that moment to return. He was carrying a black bag.

"Did the search turn up anything, Sharp?" asked

Lestrade.

"One interesting item, sir," said he, as he placed the bag on a table. "See for yourself."

Lestrade opened the bag quickly and gave a low whistle.

"Where was this found?"

"In the bedroom closet of Mrs. Thompson, sir," said Sharp.

CHAPTER FIVE

Inspector Lestrade put a hand in the bag and pulled out a brown bottle. From all appearances it was a medicine bottle. The Inspector motioned to me and I walked to his side. He handed me the bottle.

"What do you make of that, Doctor?" he asked.

"It is laudanum," I said, after a brief examination. I saw a look of strong disapproval in Lestrade's eyes. "It is not illegal, Inspector. Many people use the drug for headaches and the like."

"It may not be illegal, Doctor, but there are ten more bottles in the bag. The lady is a drug addict," said Lestrade. He turned to Sharp. "Was the bag hidden?"

"Well, yes, sir, after a fashion," said the young Yard officer. "It was under some blankets and pillows. A child could have found it."

"Perhaps a child did," said Holmes.

"Are you making a connection between this and the death of the boy?" asked Lestrade. "You think that the boy found the drug and the woman poisoned him to keep her secret?"

"It is one of the first possibilities that occurred to me. Secrets are powerful, Inspector. Once they get out, they are no longer secret."

"If she was that afraid of exposure, why not simply pour out the contents of the bottles?"

"Lestrade, really you have no concept of the mind of the addict," replied Holmes. "The destruction of her cache of drugs would be the last thing on her mind."

"It would explain much," mused the Inspector.

"Yes it would," said Holmes. "It would explain the behavior of Mr. Thompson concerning servants in the rooms. It would also explain the perpetual dreamlike state in which Mrs. Thompson walks about."

"That is true," said Lestrade. "But if I accuse her, she will certainly deny it and the husband will cause no end of trouble, I am sure."

"Let us keep this information to ourselves at present," counseled Holmes. "I would return the bag and say nothing of it for now. The fact that the Thompsons believe their secret is still intact may play in our favor."

"Very well," said Lestrade. "Sharp, are Mr. and Mrs. Thompson still in the dining room?"

"Yes, sir. As per your orders."

"Return the bag to the closet and then you may tell everyone they are free to move about."

Sharp left the room and seconds later the butler, Perkins stepped in.

"The master asks if the search is over, sir," said the man to Lestrade.

"Tell them just a bit longer and we thank them for their patience."

The butler was about to leave when Holmes halted him.

"Just a moment, Perkins," he said.

"Yes, sir," said the butler, lingering by the door.

"You have been in service to the Browns for many years."

"Yes, sir. Over twelve years, sir."

"And has there been a great deal of turnover in the staff during that time?"

"My goodness yes, sir. It is difficult to keep good people. These days every servant wants to be a tradesman. Not like when I was a lad. My father and grandfather were both butlers and I consider it a proud tradition."

"The Browns are pleasant masters?"

"Indeed, sir. Better could not be asked for."

"And their guests, the Thompsons, they are similarly pleasant?"

Perkins became aware that he had been talking rather freely with an outsider. The impassive mask of the trained servant replaced his formerly helpful demeanor.

"I am certain I would not know, sir. May I be excused?"

"Certainly, Perkins, and thank you," said Holmes.

The servant left and there remained only Lestrade, Holmes, and myself.

"I suppose we should interview the Browns," said Lestrade. Do you agree, Mr. Holmes?"

"Certainly, Inspector."

"Shall I have them brought here?"

"I rather think not, Inspector," said Holmes. "I should like to see the dining room for myself and also the kitchen, pantry, and storage room where the arsenic was kept."

This plan was agreed to and we made our way out of the library and down the hall towards the dining room. Gerald Brown darted out of a door and collided with Holmes, nearly knocking the detective off his feet.

"Slow down, my lad," said Holmes with a chuckle. "You are certainly Gerald Brown."

"I am," said the boy with a smile.

"I was just talking to your governess and she says you are a very bright young man."

The boy made no reply and simply smiled again.

"Of course," continued Holmes, "there must not be many playmates for you."

"No, I suppose not," agreed the boy.

"But you must have played with John Carpenter."

"No, sir. Mother does not hold with mixing with the servants. She says it's common."

"But Miss Hopkins says you and he were thick as thieves and played together often."

The young boy's face turned suddenly grim and he set his jaw. I, meanwhile, was flabbergasted by the bald-faced lie Holmes had told.

"She doesn't know what she is talking about," he declared. "Besides, she's terribly old and forgets things."

"Well, I suppose I can get the truth from your mother."

Holmes made as if to leave and the boy sprang in front of him, blocking the path down the hall.

"Please, sir," said the boy in a plaintive voice, "please don't tell Mother. She'll be frightfully angry."

Holmes put both hands on the boy's shoulders and spoke in a soothing voice. "I will not tell your mother, if you promise to be truthful with me. Is that a bargain?"

Holmes's manner immediately calmed the boy. Still, he glanced furtively over his shoulder for anyone who might overhear.

"It is as you say, sir," said Gerald in a whisper. "He and I used to play often when Mother was not around."

"Then you liked him," said Holmes.

"Oh yes. We were great chums. He was a good lad. We were much alike and we had lots of fun," said the boy. His face suddenly turned downcast. "But now he's gone. You don't think anyone suspects me of doing him in, do you, sir?"

"Of course not, my boy," said Holmes. "Tell me, did your sister like young John?"

"Oh, rather not," said Gerald with a grin crossing his face again. "She said he was a horrid lad and just a servant, but then again she thinks I am horrid sometimes too."

"That will be all, lad," said Holmes. "Run along and do not worry about this conversation."

Without another word Gerald scurried down the hall and turned a corner, going out of view.

"What was that business about, Mr. Holmes?" asked Lestrade.

"I wondered myself," I volunteered. To my surprise, Holmes answered right away.

"It was just an experiment to see if he would lie about it."

"But how did you know the first answer was a lie?" I asked. "The governess told you no such thing."

"It was a white lie, I assure you, Doctor."

"Still, the lad did not seem to express much sorrow for his deceased friend," observed Lestrade.

The Inspector was correct, but I gauged Gerald's attitude was an affectation of youth and not callousness. I was still pondering this as we came into the dining room. Clive and Victoria Brown were sitting at the table, but there was no sign of the Thompsons.

Clive noticed my surprise and correctly read my thoughts.

"Our American visitors dashed out of here as soon as Inspector Sharp announced the search was concluded," he said in his baritone.

I made the necessary introductions and Clive seemed ecstatic to be in the company of the great Sherlock Holmes. He grasped Holmes's hand and I thought he would never stop shaking it.

"Mr. Holmes, I feel as if I know you," he said. "It is as if a great weight has been lifted from my shoulders. I knew you were here, of course, but actually meeting you warms my heart. I am certain you will get to the bottom of this. The police," he gestured at Lestrade, "seem to think this might have been a murder attempt on my life, but that is absurd."

"Absurd or not, it is an avenue that must be explored, sir," said Holmes.

"But why would anyone want to kill me? I am a humble junior minister."

"Who profits materially by your death?" asked Lestrade bluntly.

Clive coloured slightly at the question, but mastered himself quickly. "No one does, Inspector."

"Come now," said Lestrade. "This is a fine house. It must be worth a fortune."

"That is just it, Inspector," said Clive. "The money is all Victoria's. I was as poor as a church mouse when we met. All this finery is hers. At my death, nothing would change."

I was shocked that I had overlooked this fact. Clive had lived elegantly for so long I had quite forgotten that it had not always been so.

"Even so, you may have made political enemies of which you are unaware," said Holmes.

Clive Brown seemed dubious, but he made no further effort to dissuade Holmes.

"Do you have a theory of your own, Mr. Brown?" inquired Holmes.

The question obviously took Clive by surprise and he stumbled a reply.

"Well...it is just that...well, I thought the boy may have done it himself," he stammered finally.

"Do you mean suicide?" asked Inspector Lestrade eagerly. "Had the boy discussed ending his life? This is the first I am hearing of this, I am sure."

"I don't mean exactly suicide, Inspector," said Clive. He looked to his wife helplessly.

"What my husband means, Inspector, is that he thinks that the boy poisoned the ham himself and then he planned to discover the poisoning in time to prevent anyone becoming ill," she said. "Clive explained his thoughts on this to me this morning after the doctor found it was arsenic poisoning. After some consideration, I believe he just may be right."

"And why is that, Mrs. Brown?" said Holmes. "This theory of your husband's is most intriguing."

"It is simply that the boy was most grandiose," she explained. "I blame the penny press for putting wild ideas into the lower classes."

"It is an idea," said Lestrade. "What is your thinking, Mr. Holmes?"

"It is a possibility, of course," conceded Holmes, "but just how likely it is, I cannot say at present."

Holmes lapsed into silence. His chin was lowered almost to his chest as he was in deep thought. Lestrade pulled his notebook out and was about to begin his own questioning of the Browns when Holmes clapped his hands together softly.

"Well, Lestrade, Watson and I must be off," he said.

I showed my surprise rather plainly, but I said nothing. Lestrade looked at Holmes in some confusion.

"But, Mr. Holmes, I have many more questions and I had thought that you were going to assist in the investigation," said the Inspector.

"By all means, ask your questions, Lestrade, but for myself I need to cogitate over all I have learned today. It is quite a three-pipe problem, I should think. Come along, Watson."

Before I could offer a word of protest, Holmes whisked me from the room. Once outside, my friend quickly engaged us a hansom. To my surprise, Holmes gave our destination as Charing Cross Station. As the cab rattled away from the Brown home, I looked at Holmes and saw only his usual impassive face.

"Are we to take a trip then, Holmes?" I asked.

"Regrettably, only I am taking this trip, Watson," said he.

"But I wish to see all, Holmes. Surely I can be of aid, or are you attempting to shield me from danger?"

"Nothing so melodramatic, I assure you, Doctor," he said airily. "It is simply that I must move quickly and so I go alone. With any luck I will be back before morning."

CHAPTER SIX

He would be drawn no further and the cab soon deposited him at the busy Charing Cross Station. His tall, spare form gradually disappeared among the masses. With little other choice, I gave the driver my own address.

Once safely ensconced in my chair at home, I began to ponder just what Holmes was up to. I had heard no evidence that required a train trip, but obviously my friend had.

Deciding I could do little but idly speculate upon the purpose of Holmes's journey, I began to read *The Times*. The great paper had no news, of course, of the death of an obscure servant. I wondered if that would change were it found that the famous Sherlock Holmes was investigating.

An hour later, I had exhausted the news and had nearly lapsed into a nap, when there was a sharp knock on the door. My page-boy entered, followed by Clive Brown. I sprang to my feet to shake hands with him and quickly ushered him to a chair.

Little time had elapsed since our last meeting, but the junior minister looked positively haggard.

"Are you quite yourself?" I asked, as I resumed my own chair.

"I believe that the seriousness of what had happened is only now beginning to dawn upon me," he said in a hoarse voice. "When it was first discovered that the boy, and the ham, had been poisoned, I was upset, but I thought that it must be some sort of tragic accident."

"I thought you believed the boy did it on purpose to show himself as a hero," said I.

"I don't know what I think anymore, Doctor," he said. I offered him a cigarette. He declined, opened his own cigarette case, and plucked one out. I joined him in a smoke. He took several deep drags and the tobacco seemed to soothe his jangled nerves.

"What of your wife?" I asked.

"She thinks I am at my club. I simply could not stay another moment in that house. Everyone is on edge and Victoria's cousin simply cannot shut up for one second. With all this going on, he still talks of nothing but business."

"Have you come to grips with the possibility that

you were the intended target of this crime?"

He looked at me shrewdly. "Does Mr. Holmes really have inside information that I am to be elevated?" he asked.

"As I said before, it is in the works. According to Mycroft Holmes, who is in the know as they say, you are marked for higher things," said I. "Why do you think Inspector Lestrade was assigned to the case? He is thought of as top man at Scotland Yard."

"Why, I had thought that he was interested in the case because Mr. Holmes and yourself were concerned in the matter."

"That is completely backward, my friend. It is true that his interest was piqued when he discovered that I had been to the house the previous day, but he only learned that after he was assigned the case. It was your name that ran this case to the top of the list."

Clive Brown appeared genuinely surprised by this turn of events. Before he could speak again, the door flew open and John Thompson appeared upon the threshold. He walked into the room and stood between Clive and myself.

"Am I disturbing a *tête-à-tête*?" he asked in a sneering tone. "You're plotting against me, aren't you?

The page-boy appeared at the door.

"I am sorry, Doctor," he said. "He simply rushed by me, he did."

"That is all right, Jack," said I. "You may go."

The lad withdrew with a bow. I returned my attention to John Thompson.

"Answer me," the man demanded. "I'll not be made a fool of."

"No one needs to make a fool out of you, Thompson," said Clive. "You do a bloody fine job of it yourself."

"I know a hanging party when I see one," said John Thompson.

His face was ashen and it seemed that the man was on the verge of a complete breakdown. I stood up, took him firmly by the shoulder, and guided him to a sofa. For all his bluster he gave me no resistance, and I soon thrust a snifter of brandy in his hands.

"Drink that down," I ordered, "and then we can talk as civilized men."

Thompson threw down his brandy in one toss and I saw colour coming back into his cheeks. He looked shame-faced at both Clive and myself.

"I offer my apologies to both of you," he said evenly. "I have been under tremendous pressure of late. That combined with that poor boy's death and the police pawing through my things has caused me to act quite outside of my usual manner."

It was eloquently put and I was quite willing to accept his apology. I saw at once that Clive was in agreement.

"Let us put it from our minds," I suggested. "But what is it that has brought you here?"

"Well, the fact is, after Clive left for his club, I thought I might have a few words with Mr. Holmes. He was not home, but his landlady gave me your address, Doctor. I need to talk with someone."

"Is it about the crime?" I asked.

"In a way, yes."

"Then, surely you should speak to Inspector Lestrade," I said.

"Now, Doctor, I am an old ranch hand, and I can tell who the lead bull is in the corral," Thompson said with a grin. "The Inspector was following Mr. Holmes around like a lost calf. No, Mr. Holmes is the man for me. Besides, Mr. Holmes is unofficial, if you know what I mean. And unofficial is what I want."

"I'm really not following you," I said.

"Then let me put it plainly. I know that the police found Betty's laudanum during their search," he said with a grimace. "It is an embarrassment, but not one that I would kill for. You must believe me."

"What is the connection between the drugs and the death of the boy?" asked Clive.

"The boy was snooping one day earlier this week and found the drugs. I caught him putting the bag back and chastised him for his mischief. I am afraid I quite lost my temper and threw him out of the room. Clive, your young daughter was in the hallway when it happened. When I opened the door to toss the little snoop out, she was walking by. She must have overheard all."

"She never said a thing," said Clive.

"Well, she is bound to at any minute and I wanted my side of the story told first. I didn't even know that Betty had brought the stuff with her until we were here. I have been trying to wean her off of it, but she can be cunning."

"Does she realize she has put you and herself at risk of suspicion of murder?" I asked.

"Of course not," came the reply. "She is

cunning, as I say, but it is the cunning of a child. She persists in her fiction that she takes the drug for headaches and nothing more. She does not see what any fool would see, which is that she is an addict."

I pondered this new information and wished that Holmes were here to guide me.

"And that is the sole reason you came to see Holmes?" I asked.

I saw hesitation come into the eyes of John Thompson.

"The answer to that is no, Doctor," he said finally. "The fact is that although I have told Clive and Victoria that my business thrives, the truth is that I am in dire straits. This trip was actually to see if I could persuade Clive to invest some money in my company."

"You wanted a loan from me?" asked Clive incredulously. "But you have talked of nothing else but your success."

"And that is how things were only last year. I have had some reverses in the market, but I know I will rebound, if only I have enough funds to carry me through this year. Otherwise I will have to sell all my land to cover my margin losses."

"Just a moment," I interjected. "As I understand

it, the money is Victoria's and she is your own cousin. Why not ask her directly?"

"I have, Doctor, I assure you," said Thompson. "Victoria said that the decision was Clive's and that if he agreed, she would not stand in the way. I was trying to work up the courage to ask Clive when this rotten business happened. I am afraid if it all comes out that it will look black for Betty and me. That is why I came here. To put myself in Mr. Holmes's hands and ask for his help."

"That is an interesting tale, Mr. Thompson," said I. "And I can sympathize with your desire for discretion, but surely you can see that this information must be given to the authorities."

"But I had hoped..." began Thompson, but I raised my hand to stop him.

"Surely you must see how this will look if it is discovered by Scotland Yard instead of volunteered by you."

"But they will already be suspicious that I tried to hide it."

"That they will," I conceded, "but you still have time to redeem yourself before it is too late. Besides, I have worked many cases with Holmes and with Scotland Yard, and they realize that people hold back critical information for many reasons other than guilt of a crime. Go to Lestrade and tell him what you have told me. As you say, they already know of the laudanum."

"I'll do it," said the American with sudden resolution. "Well, I have taken up too much of your time, Dr. Watson, and I have intruded upon a private conversation. I will take my leave."

He made as if to rise, but Clive stayed his movement with a gesture.

"How much money do you need?" Clive asked.

"Why, perhaps as much as twenty thousand dollars."

"Then you shall have it," said Clive. "After all, John, we are family and blood is thicker than water."

I had not heard Clive use the man's Christian name before that moment. I wondered if the American appreciated how big a step that informality was.

"Clive, I couldn't ask you for it now," Thompson protested.

"You are not asking, I am offering. Let us consider it an investment. Will that meet with your approval?"

"Indeed it will!" said Thompson with

appreciation.

The American's spirits were so brightened that I wondered if he had forgotten that he was facing a visit to Scotland Yard and some undoubtedly difficult questions from Inspector Lestrade. After a few more minutes of shaking hands with Clive and myself, John Thompson bid us goodbye and left. I could hear him whistling an unfamiliar, yet happy tune as the door closed behind him.

"That ended somewhat differently than it began," I said.

"You know, Watson, I believe that deep down he is really a good fellow. It was his bluster that I could not get past. Perhaps that was all a cover for the reduced circumstances he finds himself in."

"You made him a handsome offer to invest in his company, when he would have settled for a loan," said I.

"Ah, but, Watson, the tax implications are much better should the money be lost than if it were a mere loan," Clive said with a grin.

I had not thought Clive to be such a man of business to be aware of such things, but I reminded myself that I was much better acquainted with the Clive of youth than the middle-aged man before me.

We shared several more cigarettes over the next hour, before Clive declared that he must also leave. I walked him out to the street and saw him off. Once back in my comfortable sitting room, I glanced at the clock and wondered again just where Holmes had gone.

CHAPTER SEVEN

I received no word from Holmes that night. The next morning I arose somewhat earlier than was my habit. I had hoped to find a telegram awaiting me, but it was not to be. I had a solitary breakfast and settled down in the sitting room to see what the day might bring. The morning papers were still silent on the poisoning. It was near mid-morning when Holmes unexpectedly arrived at my home.

"Hello, Watson," said he as he came in. "I see you have had your breakfast, but no matter. I will have a cup of coffee."

"Holmes, I did not hold breakfast because I had no idea that you were going to be here this morning. You have kept me in the dark," I reminded him. "Were I in your confidence perhaps I could plan better."

"No matter, old friend," said he airily.

"I take it from your manner that your trip was successful."

"Indeed, Doctor. It was most illuminating. I

always find a train trip quite invigorating."

"Perhaps then you will include me in your illumination," I said.

"That is a very well-turned phrase, Doctor. I sense that I have bruised your feelings somewhat, so I will tell you where I have been. I took the train from Charing Cross yesterday to Chelmsford."

"Chelmsford! Whatever for?" I asked.

"Doctor, you state the name as if you have never heard it before," scoffed Holmes.

"I have heard of the town, of course, but I see no connection to the case. Wait half a moment," I said as it suddenly came to me. "Chelmsford was where John Carpenter's mother opened her seamstress shop.

"Very good, Doctor."

"But what could you hope to find there that would have any bearing on the events at the Brown's home?"

"Firstly, I wished to verify that she did actually settle there."

"Did you doubt it?"

"It is always best to make certain, Doctor.

Secondly there were certain details that I wished to confirm to my satisfaction."

"I take it you went there with a theory of the case in mind."

"Indeed I did."

"And the facts in Chelmsford must have borne out whatever theory you have constructed."

"That is so."

"Then the case is solved."

"I believe that I can join all the strings together at this point," said Holmes. "I see that you have had a least one guest in my absence."

"That is so, but how could you determine that fact?"

"It is a simple deduction, my friend. I observe that the ashtray has not only your Bradley brand, but also other unmarked stubs. Therefore, you have had a guest."

"Those stubs could be days old, Holmes."

Oh no, Doctor," said he. "The good Mrs. Watson has a better-trained staff than that. These stubs are from last night at the latest."

"In any event, you are correct. I have had a guest and in fact I had two guests," I said. I went on to explain that the visitors had been Clive Brown and John Thompson. Holmes listened attentively as I related all that had been said in his absence.

"Interesting, Watson. So the American millionaire was actually here in England with his hat in his hand," said Holmes, as I concluded.

"More like with his hand out, I should say, Holmes."

"I must say that this adds several new elements to the case," said he.

"Does this disarrange your theory of the case, Holmes?" I asked.

"Not in the main. Though it does ruffle the edges, but then again, murder is an untidy business."

"Then it was murder, and not a game gone wrong, as Clive Brown supposed possible."

"This was no game, Watson. It was calculated, premeditated murder. A child has died at the hand of a cold-blooded poisoner."

Holmes suggested we return to Baker Street and I acquiesced. And a short time later we were in those humble quarters. Holmes had said nothing of the case on the way. He looked over some correspondence that had arrived in his absence and then sat. Lighting his pipe, he leaned back in his chair.

I had hoped that Holmes was about to expound upon his thinking, when there was a knock at the door and Inspector Lestrade walked in. There were polite greetings all around and the Inspector sat down. He had a somber expression on his face.

"What brings you here this morning, Inspector?" asked Holmes.

"Bad tidings, Mr. Holmes, I am sorry to say," replied Lestrade. "There has been another death."

My thoughts immediately flew to my friend.

"Has Clive been killed, Inspector?" I asked.

"No, Doctor. The servant, Judith Barnes, has died."

"Lestrade, I notice you say died and death, but not murder," observed Holmes. "Will you elaborate, please?"

"The girl was found dead at the foot of the back stairs by the cook."

"The cook again," murmured Holmes.

"By all appearances she fell down the steps and broke her neck," said Lestrade. "The doctor says that death was instantaneous. There were no marks of violence upon her save those from the fall. On another day or in another house I might call it an accident, but in that house only a day after the boy..."

The Inspector left his thought unfinished, but it was not necessary that he finish. His thoughts were my own and I was certain also that Holmes felt the same way. This was almost certainly another deliberate killing.

"Did no one hear anything in the night?" asked Holmes.

"No, sir. It was a windy night, and the house is quite large. Perhaps it was an accident."

"No, Inspector, your first instinct was correct," said Holmes.

"Then this is a murder."

"Yes, it is murder, and murder committed to cover up for the killing of John Carpenter. Not a crime as carefully planned as the first one and certainly more reckless, but murder nonetheless."

Lestrade looked troubled.

"I have come here, Mr. Holmes, because I am no nearer solving this case than when we began. What with this second death, the pressure from above to come to a solution is enormous, I don't mind telling you."

"Then take comfort in the fact that I know who the murderer is," said Holmes.

"Who is it, sir?" asked the Inspector.

"I ask that you not press me at this moment, Inspector. I need some time to formulate just how to trap the killer."

"Then it is possible the killer may still escape justice, Holmes?" I asked.

"The evidence is tenuous and circumstantial. What I know may not be enough to convict if the culprit attempts to brazen it out," said Holmes. "However, I should be able to devise a way in which to bring maximum pressure to bear."

I could see that the Inspector was not satisfied by that response. From my long association with the great detective, I had learned that he had his own methods and would rarely vary them for anyone, even Scotland Yard. Lestrade knew this as well, and he choked back any threats that may have been on his tongue.

"What is your program then, Mr. Holmes?" he asked. "May I at least be privy to that?"

Holmes quietly lit a pipe. He took several deep

puffs before he answered. "Inspector, I realize that I cannot expect your patience to be infinite. Let us arrange to meet at the Brown residence this evening at eight. At that time I will reveal the killer. With any luck you shall have not only my word, but also a confession."

"You will need luck, you say, Mr. Holmes?" asked a clearly skeptical Lestrade.

"Normally luck is just good preparation disguised, as I have said before, but I admit that luck will play a role. How large I cannot say. I can say that I am confident that with the hours before we meet at the Brown residence this evening, I will be ready to present my case."

"You know, of course, that Mr. John Thompson came to Scotland Yard yesterday with an interesting tale," said Lestrade.

"The Doctor has told me that Mr. Thompson planned to do so, but I had not known that he did before your statement. What do you think of Thompson's story?"

"I do not know what to think. He must have known we found the drugs, so perhaps he felt that he had no choice but to come clean. It does provide a motive for killing the boy, I suppose. His wife's habit is not illegal even if it might be embarrassing. People have killed for less."

"That is certainly true, Lestrade. Secrets take on a life of their own and the guardians of those secrets can sometimes impart exaggerated importance to those secrets."

"You are right, Holmes," said I. "We have seen more than our share of such cases."

"This talk does not advance the case in my opinion, so I shall be off."

The Inspector arose and began to leave.

"Before you go, Inspector," began Holmes, "I request that all of the principals of the house be present, including the butler and the cook."

"It will be as you say, sir," said Lestrade.

With those words he left, and Holmes and I were alone again. I was shaken a bit by the death of the servant girl. I had faith in Holmes, but I worried about Clive. If this was a political conspiracy then he could still be in peril. I assumed that Lestrade had men at the Brown house, so I supposed there would be no danger, as long as Holmes exposed the killer before another nightfall.

Holmes was quietly smoking his pipe with his feet curled up beside him on the sofa. The languid picture would have led the inexperienced watcher to assume that Holmes was in repose, but I knew it to be an indicator of immense intellectual activity.

Although I was no longer in residence at Baker Street I resolved to stay the day through, if Holmes voiced no objections. I had no patients for the day, and I did not relish returning to my lonely home. I had passed an hour reading a history on the War of the Roses, when Holmes finally broke his silence.

"Doctor, I admire your ability to remain silent when I know that curiosity abounds within your breast," said he. "It is a side of your personality that doubtless traces back to your military training."

It was also a result of long association with the great detective. I knew that questions would not be answered even if asked and that the best way to get Holmes to speak was to wait him out. A wearisome process at best, yet one I knew to be effective.

"Have you determined on how to proceed tonight at the Browns?" I asked.

"I have, Watson. I admit that this second death has surprised me. I did not think the culprit to be so desperate as to strike again. It only goes to demonstrate how murder can darken the soul. The second murder is always easier than the first."

"Why was the second murder committed, if I

may ask?"

"It was to cover the first murder, of course," said Holmes in reply.

"Do you mean to say the girl witnessed the first murder? Why did she not come forward?"

"She was a witness, Doctor, but not of murder."

It was a baffling reply. I would have followed up with more questions, but Holmes resumed his previous posture and closed his eyes as he puffed on his pipe. This was the signal, of course, that he would be drawn no further at that point.

I decided to return to my book and thus pass the time until the appointed hour. I resolved I would not leave the side of Sherlock Holmes until the double killer was exposed. I impatiently waited until we would leave for our meeting.

CHAPTER EIGHT

At half past seven, Holmes retired to his bedchamber. When he returned, I took it as the signal that we were ready to depart. We shared a mostly silent cab ride to the Brown home. All Holmes would say was that all was in order and the snare was set.

As we arrived at the house, I saw that a small knot of gawkers was still present. A uniformed sergeant stood guard at the gate to the walkway to the house. He allowed us to pass and I spied Inspector Lestrade standing just outside the doorframe of the entrance. He solemnly greeted us as we approached.

"All has been made ready as you have asked, Mr. Holmes," he said. "Sharp is inside with all of them, and they are waiting in the library.

We were ushered into the library. I immediately saw that Clive and Victoria Brown were seated on one sofa while John and Betty Thompson were seated opposite them on another. Perkins, the butler, was stationed by the entrance. He had his usual ramrod-straight posture. The cook, Emma Barton, stood somewhat ill at ease by the fireplace. It was plain that she felt out of place when not in her kitchen.

I had expected John Thompson's usual bluster when we walked in, but he seemed most pensive and merely nodded at our entrance. His wife sat primly with her hands folded on her lap. Her usual dreamy attitude had vanished and she appeared very alert. Perhaps the events of the last several days had shocked her out of her drug-induced trance.

Victoria Brown likewise seemed alert and on edge. My friend Clive leaped to his feet and greeted Holmes and myself with a grim look.

"Mr. Holmes," he said, shaking hands with both of us, "I hope you can shed some light on this madness. To think that two short days ago I was happy and my future seemed bright. Now..."

He let the thought fade to nothing. Holmes assured Clive that there would be a resolution to this business. Clive gave a weak smile in return and resumed his seat. Holmes took a position in the center of the room.

"I appreciate you all being here tonight so that I can speak with you," he said.

"We had little choice," said John Thompson. "The Inspector," he gestured towards Lestrade, "was most insistent."

"Nevertheless, I do thank you. As you know, death had struck this house twice in as many days. Young John Carpenter has been poisoned and Judith Barnes has been killed in a fall. Both were premeditated murder."

I heard a gasp escape from several in attendance.

"Surely not Judith, Mr. Holmes," cried Victoria Brown. "You just said it was a fall. I still think that the boy poisoned himself through misadventure, and if that's true, then Judith's fall could also be an accident. Don't you think so, Clive?"

Her husband merely shrugged his shoulders in a helpless gesture.

"Mr. Holmes, you did promise me that you know who the culprit is," Inspector Lestrade reminded him.

"So I did, Lestrade. Let me first describe my thinking in this case. The day of the luncheon, my friend Dr. Watson and I were discussing the prospects of Mr. Clive Brown. He is a junior minister now, but he is seen as a rising man. That night after the luncheon a young servant boy, one John Carpenter, is poisoned with food that was going to be served at breakfast. Now, who was to be at that breakfast? Only four people; the Browns and the Thompsons. The immediate thought is that Clive Brown was the intended target. The Thompsons are American visitors and Mrs. Brown has no known enemies, but Mr. Brown might have made enemies, even if he were unaware of doing so. At any rate, Scotland Yard is interested and I become involved as well through my friend Dr. Watson. The next night another servant, Judith Barnes, dies from a fall down the stairs. Are the deaths connected or is it a dreadful coincidence?

"There is a curious thing about both of these deaths. Emma Barton, the cook, is with the boy when he dies and she discovers the girl in the morning. Miss Barton even goes so far as to make a statement to the effect that she tried to give the boy a purgative. What if she gave the boy the purgative and it contained the arsenic? She could then poison the ham to make it seem as if someone was trying to kill her master, when in reality she had killed the boy for reasons of her own. Judith Barnes sees something that causes her to be suspicious of Miss Barton, so the next night the cook arranges the accident. It could have all happened just like that, and while we were chasing a non-existent political murderer, she escapes justice."

The colour had completely drained from Emma Barton's face as Holmes made the potential case against her. She reached for the fireplace mantel as if she might faint.

"It is a lie," she finally managed to croak. "I loved John Carpenter as if he were my own son, and Judith was like a daughter to me. Mr. Brown, it is not true."

Clive Brown looked with pity at the gaunt older woman. At length he gave his attention to Holmes.

"Mr. Holmes, Emma Barton has been a trusted servant of mine for almost two decades. She has been here longer than anyone. What motive would she have to kill the two deceased?"

"None that I can see, Mr. Brown," replied Holmes.

"None?" sputtered Inspector Lestrade. "Do you mean to say that Emma Barton killed twice for no reason at all?"

"No, Inspector. The deaths had a motive, but Emma Barton did not kill anyone."

"Then, what is the meaning of this charade?" asked the Inspector.

"It had a purpose, you must trust me. My point was that with a little sleight of hand, a murder could seem to be something that it is not."

"Forcing the card," I said.

"Exactly, Doctor," replied Holmes. "Take the case of Mr. Thompson. He comes upon you yesterday, Watson. Coincidentally his cousin by marriage is there also. He makes a confession. He forces the card by making everyone concentrate on what he has confessed and both matters are relatively trivial. His wife has an unpleasant habit that he wishes to conceal and he finds himself in financial straits. But what do those two confessions really tell us?

"The matter of his wife's habit, we already knew about from the search. As to the financial straits, Mr. Thompson had already broached his cousin on the subject of a loan. Neither are, strictly speaking, secrets. Yet, Mr. Thompson lends credibility to the tale by relating an incident with John Carpenter that was overheard, at least partly, by the youngest daughter of the Browns, Catherine."

"That is all true, Mr. Holmes," said Thompson in a perplexed tone of voice. "Dr. Watson counseled me to go to the authorities and I did. What more do you expect of me? I apologize if my secrets were not dark enough for you."

"I agree," said Clive Brown, coming to the edge of his seat. "John came forward in a manly way. I see no reason to badger him about it now. Surely we have more important matters at hand."

"I am afraid, Mr. Thompson, that you have missed the point of forcing the card," said Holmes.

"You can speak plainer than that, Mr. Holmes," said Inspector Lestrade. "Just what are you driving at?"

"I will tell you. Whose word do we have that the confrontation with John Carpenter was about the laudanum? Why, only John Thompson's, of course. The boy is dead and the other witness is a twelve-year-old girl who heard only the angry denunciations at the end. Imagine the fight was about something else."

"What else, Holmes?" I asked. "What else could the boy have discovered?"

"Perhaps he uncovered a plot to kill his master and to make the crime look like a political one," said Holmes. John Thompson said nothing, but was clearly stunned. "A furious Mr. Thompson throws the boy out of his room, but then thinks that he must silence the boy permanently."

"This is all poppycock," said Thompson. "Inspector, I implore you."

"I am willing to let Mr. Holmes speak, for now," said Lestrade in answer to the American. "Go on, Mr. Holmes."

"He poisons the boy by contaminating the ham.

In some manner he sees that the boy eats a portion of it, but the girl Judith suspects him. He lures her to a meeting, perhaps drugs her with laudanum, of which he has an ample supply, and kills her, too. He now makes his confession and Mr. Brown is so shaken by events and impressed by the straightforward account that he gives the man the money he seeks. Mr. Thompson takes no further action, as his purpose for coming to England has been successfully concluded."

"But, what is the motive for killing Clive?" I asked. I saw Lestrade nodding as I spoke. "He came to seek a loan from Clive. How does murdering him advance that?"

"You make a mistake, Doctor," said Holmes. "Thompson sought the loan from his cousin. Remember that Mr. Brown has little money of his own. Thompson asks Mrs. Brown, but to his surprise she defers to her husband. Mr. Thompson has pretended that he was unaware that Clive Brown disliked him, but I do not believe that. Thompson is a clever man and he can see that Clive Brown does not care for his brash manner. But what would happen if Clive Brown were dead? Why, the decision on the loan would go back to his cousin, and he has every reason to believe that she will grant his request. He had an entire empire teetering on the edge. He would have gone to any length to save it. By accident Clive Brown survives and two servants who overheard or saw the wrong thing are killed. Mr. Thompson leaves the country with twenty thousand dollars and no one is the wiser. Only questions will be left and no answers. It is possible that Clive Brown's theory that the boy accidentally poisoned himself will come to be accepted as the correct answer. In that light, it becomes much more likely that Judith Barnes's death was simply an accident as well."

As Holmes was finishing his statement, I saw Clive begin to interrupt him and then change his mind. Victoria Brown was trembling under a great emotion. She looked at her cousin with scorn.

"John, how could you do such a thing?" she asked coldly. "I always knew that you were ruthless. It is your behavior that has driven your wife into a lifetime of drugs, but I did not think you capable of murder. Two young lives snuffed out because you had to save your petty timber fortune. We share the same grandfather. He was a knight, and now look at what you have become."

"Mr. Holmes, how much of this do you know and how much is mere surmise?" asked Inspector Lestrade. "The details seem quite sketchy in my opinion."

"It is made up out of whole cloth," said Betty Thompson.

It was the first time she had spoken since we

had entered the room and all turned toward her.

"Can't you see that Mr. Holmes does not believe a word of it himself?" she continued. "He reminds me of a hunter sending the hounds into the brush to flush out the game. I am not blind to my husband's deficiencies, but murder is beyond the pale."

Holmes's face was like stone as the woman began her statement, but gradually I saw a smile begin to creep through.

"I see a first-rate mind has been dulled by the drugs, but it is not buried completely," said he in reply. "I had two reasons to accuse your husband. Firstly, I believe him to be an unscrupulous man who came here to defraud his cousin, if he could. And secondly, I wished to see just how ruthless the real killer is. I have that answer now."

CHAPTER NINE

I expected an uproar to ensue at Holmes's words, but instead the room was enveloped in silence. Holmes finally broke the stillness.

"I have outlined two possibilities in this case, but neither one explains all the facts. To do that, we have to go back to when John Carpenter's mother was in service here. She left service to open a seamstress shop in Chelmsford. There her son was born. When she died the boy came back here to go into service for the Browns.

"The year that she left has been a subject of dispute. Mrs. Brown told Dr. Watson that the woman departed twenty years ago, but when I questioned the cook, she stated that the woman left fifteen years ago. That discrepancy is important."

"She is mistaken, Mr. Holmes," said Victoria Brown clearly. "I do not see the importance of it, but it was twenty years."

"Do you remember, Mr. Brown?" asked Holmes.

"I barely remember the woman at all, Mr.

Holmes," said Clive Brown. "I certainly do not remember when she left."

"You see, Mr. Holmes," said Victoria. "One person remembers one way, another remembers another, and yet a third person remembers not at all."

"Miss Barton, how long have you been in service here?" asked Holmes.

"Why, eighteen years, sir."

"And you were in service with John Carpenter's mother when she was here?"

"That is so, sir."

"Could it be any plainer?" asked Holmes.

"What is the difference in a few years?" asked Lestrade.

"The difference is that if the cook has only been in service to the Browns for eighteen years, then she could not possibly have known the mother if the mother left twenty years ago. The timeline is very important, Inspector," said Holmes. "And memories are beside the point. I only bring the point up to demonstrate that someone has tried to confuse the issue. I went to Chelmsford by train yesterday. I have seen deed records that show that the mother moved to Chelmsford fifteen years ago and I have seen birth records that show that

John Carpenter was born some seven months later."

"Holmes, are you suggesting that the girl became with child while she was in service here?"

"Yes, Doctor. I spoke to several old neighbors and customers of the lady yesterday. They said she spoke of a husband who had died in India, but of course, that was a cover for the real story, which she could not tell."

"Are you accusing me of fathering a child out of wedlock with a servant, Mr. Holmes?" asked Clive Brown angrily as he stood up from the sofa.

"That is precisely what I am accusing you of, sir. There were three people aware of the affair, but only two knew of the child. Do you still wish to deny the affair?"

Clive met eyes with Holmes and turned to his wife. He slowly collapsed back down on the sofa.

"It is true, Mr. Holmes. I was a terrible husband as a young man, but I swear that I have made amends a thousand times over. And I swear I did not know John Carpenter was my son, if indeed he was."

"I am following you so far, Mr. Holmes," said Lestrade. "But if the affair was so long ago, how could it be the cause of a crime today?"

Those were my thoughts as well and I listened carefully for Holmes to answer. If he was accusing my friend Clive of this crime, I was going to need to be persuaded.

"The answer lies in biology, Inspector," replied Holmes. "Remember we have to account for the murder of Judith Barnes as well."

"Biology?" I repeated woodenly.

"Yes, Doctor. You were the witness to the impetus of the two murders. You saw and heard what set this in motion."

"When, Holmes?" I asked.

"I asked you to relate every conversation that you had the day of the luncheon. You did so quite well, but I was particularly interested in your interaction with the boy in question, since he would die half a day later."

"But I had little interaction with him, Holmes. He broke a dish, but he barely spoke the entire time, except to apologize for the accident."

"Doctor, was the boy in the adolescent stage of life?" asked Holmes.

"Yes," I said. "At age fourteen, that would accurately describe it."

"What changes take place as the adolescent boy comes into manhood?"

"Well, he begins growing facial hair and certain...err...drives come into play," I said with embarrassment.

"Does the voice change?"

"Oh, of course, it does, Holmes."

"And did not the boy's voice crack and change during his apology?"

"Yes, it did," I replied. I began to see what Holmes was driving at. The voice of the boy that day changed into one I knew well. I was shocked that I had missed it at the time.

"The voice of the son is often much like the voice of the father," continued Holmes. "Physical likenesses can be put down to chance. Many people are the same build and have the same hair colour, but the voice of a father to son can be an uncanny indicator of parentage. The boy's voice broke that day into a baritone for a few moments. Three people noticed at once how alike the voice was to Clive Brown."

"Three people, Holmes?" said I. "There were only four people in the room, counting the boy, and I am afraid that I did not notice the similarity at the time."

"You forget Gerald Brown, Doctor," said Holmes.

"He wasn't even in the room. He came in a few seconds later," I replied.

"Exactly, Doctor, and what did he say?"

"Well, as I recall, he said he thought that his father was in the room."

"And why do you think that was?" asked Holmes. "The reason is obvious. He thought he heard his father's voice. Victoria Brown was quick to recognize this. She reprimanded him as she had reprimanded Judith Barnes. Doctor, you had thought that the girl laughed at John Carpenter because of the accident, but in reality she, too, recognized that the son had revealed himself. Perhaps there has even been some gossip about this in the servant quarters prior to the incident in question."

Holmes shot a glance at Perkins, but the butler remained impassive. However, the face of Emma Barton told a different tale. The cook's cheeks burned with crimson under Holmes's glare. It was obvious that his arrow had struck home.

"What say you, Miss Barton?" asked Holmes. "Has there been such talk among the staff?"

"I am sure that I do not know," she answered. I admired her loyalty, misplaced though it seemed.

"That will not do," growled Lestrade. "This is a murder investigation and I demand you answer the question Mr. Holmes has put to you."

"I will not repeat gossip," said the cook with determination.

"So there is gossip to repeat," observed Holmes. "That answers the question quite nicely."

"So, now you accuse me, Mr. Holmes," said Victoria Brown. "You are an incautious man. Such words lodged against my cook or my cousin may be simply injudicious, but against me they may be both slanderous and actionable. I may see you in court."

"You may very well see me in court, madam," said Holmes.

"So your theory is that Mrs. Brown recognized the voice of the maturing boy to be that of her husband and then she decided to murder the lad," said the Inspector.

"Certainly not, Lestrade," returned Holmes. "As I said, three people knew of the affair, but only two people knew of the child. When she discovered she was with child the mother approached Mrs. Brown. She then decided that the only way to avoid a scandal was for the mother to leave. Mrs. Brown bundled the woman off with enough money to open her small shop and the problem was solved for the moment. However, Victoria Brown was a careful woman and she kept a watch over the bastard son of her husband. When his mother became ill and died she decided to keep him where she could control him."

"Meaning that she brought him back here as a servant," said I.

"When she realized what she must do, she made you believe that bringing John Carpenter back here had been her husband's idea. Is that so, Mr. Brown?" asked Holmes. "Did you suggest bringing the Carpenter boy into service in the house?"

"Why, no, I did not," he said in a shaken voice. "I admit the affair, but I was being truthful when I said I barely remembered the girl. I just remember that she left and I was relieved. I knew of no child, and I certainly did not ask to have him brought here."

"A lie from Victoria Brown," said Holmes. "Mr. Brown, your wife advanced a theory that she said came from you. It was a theory that the boy had accidentally poisoned himself. Was that your idea, as she said?"

"Well...in fact...no...no it wasn't," the man stammered. "She suggested it to me."

"Another lie," said Holmes. "So now we have a strong motive for murder. Victoria Brown does not want the old family secret to become known. Especially as her husband is marked for a possible Cabinet post. She decides on poison. She knows that arsenic is kept in a storeroom off the kitchen and she doses the ham with it. She then not only has to poison the boy, but to do so in a manner that will implicate the ham at once. Otherwise she will have to come up with a reason not to let anyone eat it the next day at breakfast. One matter which has been overlooked so far is how did the plate of poisoned ham come to be in the boy's room?"

"The murderer brought it to the room certainly, Mr. Holmes," said Lestrade.

"Yes, Inspector, but who would be likely to do that? The boy knew it was forbidden to the staff, so who would he have accepted the plate from? Why not from his mistress? Mrs. Brown is the very person who brought him to the home and gave him employment. It would be ungracious not to accept the food. He would never think anything was wrong. He died from his innocence.

"The plan has worked. The threat is gone, and even though the police are investigating, there seems no real danger. And then there is Judith Barnes. What was it? Did the girl intimate knowledge of the parentage of the boy? Remember, Victoria Brown heard the laugh when the boy's voice broke. Whatever the reason, the girl is hurled down the stairs and dies as well. Is that a close approximation of the events, Mrs. Brown?"

The lady stared at Holmes for a long minute.

"It was a fanciful account, if I may say," she finally replied. "I rather think you have missed your calling, Mr. Holmes. You should write for the theatre. First you accuse my cook and my own cousin, and now I am the target. It is a very scattershot approach."

"It had a logical order, madam, I assure you," said Holmes. "I made the case against your cook and your cousin in order to gauge your reaction, and that reaction was instructive. When I made the case against the cook you recognized it as mere fluff, as did Mrs. Thompson, and you smiled. However, when I made the more convincing case against your cousin you decided to join in and help sink him. You lashed out against him in order to divert suspicion away from yourself and onto an innocent, if not entirely trustworthy, man. By doing so, you have unveiled yourself as a ruthless and remorseless killer."

"You may have convinced yourself of that, Mr. Holmes," she replied acidly, "and even the Inspector, but do you think you can convince twelve Englishmen of my guilt with such evidence?"

"It was not my hope to convince twelve Englishmen," said Holmes softly. "I only hoped to convince one. Look at him, madam. I think you will see that I have done that."

Holmes motioned towards Clive Brown and I saw the horror on his face. Victoria Brown reached for him and he shrank back as if from a diseased hand.

"Victoria," he said in a whisper. "The cruelty."

"Clive, you don't mean to say you believe this man," said she. "He is a charlatan, a deceiver."

"No," said Clive with growing strength. "It is you who are the deceiver. You lied about who brought John back here. You lied about when his mother left. You put that silly theory about the boy poisoning himself in my mouth when it was your idea. And all of this to cover up an illegitimate child? Victoria, kings have had bastards and still ruled England."

"You are not a king, you fool! You are a little man being propped up by my money and my grandfather's lineage. Do you think you would be under consideration for the Cabinet were it not for me? You disgust me with your lack of ambition. You would have taken in the boy as your oldest son if you had learned the truth. You would have shamed Gerald and Catherine. That is why I had to take action. To save you and to save this family."

"Then you admit the killing, madam?" asked

Holmes softly.

"Yes, I killed the boy. He would have destroyed our lives. It had to be done."

"And the girl, too?"

"Yes," she replied, but her tone became wistful. "The boy deserved to die, but Judith was just a stupid girl."

"Did she threaten to expose you?" asked Holmes.

"Hardly that," said Victoria Brown, and she barked a bitter laugh. "If you can believe it, she came to me and gave me her word that she would remain silent. Her word? Can you believe the gall? She proposed to give me her word as if we were social equals. The very idea."

She laughed again and this time it took on an hysterical tone. I shot a glance at Holmes. He was stone-faced, but I feared for the woman's sanity. Lestrade walked to the woman's side.

"You must come with me to Scotland Yard, Mrs. Brown," he said in an officious tone.

The lady arose with dignity, and without a word to anyone, she left with the Inspector.

CHAPTER TEN

The next day I breakfasted with Sherlock Holmes at 221B Baker Street. Holmes, as was his habit, did not discuss the recent case during our meal. However, he informed me that Inspector Lestrade and Clive Brown were expected that morning, and that he would satisfy any curiosity about the investigation at that time when all were present.

Inspector Lestrade arrived first and was enjoying a cigar, when a somber Clive Brown came in. I greeted my friend and soon he was seated with a cup of strong coffee.

"Mr. Holmes," said Clive, "I cannot say I am happy with the manner in which the investigation was ended, but I am grateful that you found the reason behind this insanity."

"I believe insanity is the right word," said I. "I would surmise that the years of carrying that secret drove Victoria mad. She was not in possession of her faculties."

"Are you testifying as a medical expert, Doctor?"

asked a bemused Lestrade.

"It is my personal opinion, Inspector, and not a medical one. Though I daresay that avenue will be explored by her solicitor."

"Perhaps, Doctor," said the Inspector, "but the lady does not seem inclined to aid in her defense. She has not spoken a word since she was taken into custody."

"It is true," said Clive. "I attempted to see her this morning before I came here. She would not speak with me at all. I am not certain she even knew I was there. Very sad."

"Remember the good woman she was, old friend," I said.

Clive was visibly struggling with his emotions. He arose from his seat and faced Holmes.

"Mr. Holmes," he said, "I came this morning to thank you for your work, but I cannot remain. I have funeral services to see to. I must bury a son who I never knew to be my child in life. I fear I may never put down the burden I carry in my mind. This was partially my fault, after all."

With those cryptic words, Clive Brown took his leave. Once he had left, I put a question to Holmes.

"What do you suppose he meant about being partially at fault?" I asked.

"He was merely acknowledging the obvious, Doctor," replied Holmes. "His illicit affair of fifteen years past lit a slow fuse that finally ignited a powder keg. Clive Brown is certainly not guilty of murder, but he carries the stain of his sin that began the chain of events."

"So you knew that John Carpenter was Clive Brown's son since the beginning, is that it Mr. Holmes?" asked Lestrade. "Mighty close of you to guard that knowledge from the Yard."

"I suspected it, Lestrade," said Holmes, "but I was not certain until I went to Chelmsford to verify it."

"But when did you first suspect the lineage of the boy?" I asked.

"Why, Doctor, it occurred to me as a possibility before you even attended the luncheon at the Brown's home."

"Before? There was no crime to be concerned with at that point, and you had no way of knowing John Carpenter even existed," said I. "How could you suspect anything at that early date?"

"Perhaps suspect is too strong of a word, Doctor," Holmes conceded. "What I can say is that you mentioned what a rascal, to use your phrase, Clive Brown had been in his early married days. I remember musing about what the wives of such men have to submit themselves to. The idea of illegitimate children even then ran through my mind, and when the boy was murdered, it occurred to me again."

"That was a rather wild theory, Holmes, if you don't mind my saying so."

"It was nothing set in stone, I assure you. However, you then related the tale of the boy's voice changing. The reaction of those in the room and that of Gerald Brown outside the room, struck me rather forcefully. It was then that I suspected Victoria Brown."

"But why Victoria Brown and not Clive Brown?" asked Lestrade. "It might have been either one trying to keep the secret of the boy's parentage."

"Yes," agreed Holmes, "except that Victoria Brown immediately told Watson a lie about the boy's mother. That guided my hand. It was also the manner of the boy's death that pointed towards his mistress rather than his master. Victoria Brown could easily wander through the kitchen and the pantry and not arouse suspicion. After all, she runs the household, but could Clive Brown, or any man, move about in these areas without causing comment? I think not."

"What was that business with Gerald Brown

about?" I asked. "What was so important about whether or not he and John Carpenter played together?"

"It was a minor point, Doctor, but it was another thread. It went to Victoria Brown's state of mind. There was a strange dichotomy at play here. On one hand she hated the existence of John Carpenter, but with the other hand she drew him back to the home.

"She could have allowed him to wallow in poverty after the death of his mother, but she brought him back into her own house. At first, I am certain that she did so to see if the lad had any idea who his father was. Once she determined he did not know, she could have dismissed him, but she did not. Her compulsion to control the boy kept him in her service, but she did not want the two half-brothers to associate with one another. They might begin to realize the secret. Remember that Gerald Brown said he and Carpenter had much in common. At any rate, I found it interesting to gauge just how upset Gerald Brown might be if I implied that his mother found he had disobeyed her. As you saw, he was terrified by the notion."

"It still seems quite thin, Holmes," I groused. "A jury might never have convicted the lady had she not confessed."

"That is why I had to accuse the cousin, Mr. John Thompson," said Holmes. "It occurred to me that a woman who would kill for her husband would collapse if he turned against her. It was essential to lay out the case for her being the killer not to her, but to her husband."

"You felt that she would break down if he thought her guilty?" asked Lestrade.

"Precisely," said Holmes, clapping his hands together. "Once the immense cruelty of the crimes was brought to his attention and placed at the foot of his wife, Clive Brown made the decision I had hoped he would make. Faced with his horror at the blood on her hands, all pretense fell away."

"It was a lucky chance that she did confess, Holmes," said I.

"It was all done according to a plan, Doctor, but many times what appears to be luck is merely hard work and intelligence disguised."

"Of course, Holmes," I said with a smile, "but you will admit that the fact that I heard the boy's voice change was luck."

"I would have been kinder than that, Doctor, but have it your way. Your part in this case was pure luck with no intelligent direction."

That was not at all what I had meant, and Holmes knew it, but I decided to let the matter drop.

Lestrade chuckled at my discomfort and rose to leave.

"I have a busy day ahead, gentlemen. If you will excuse me," he said.

Goodbyes were exchanged and again, I found myself alone with Holmes in the sitting room of what was once our humble bachelor quarters. I looked at the clock and realized that I too must soon take my leave. Holmes was curled up in his chair, with his pipe, a halo of smoke circled around his head. I was on the point of telling Holmes that I must return to my home, when he stirred.

"I say, Watson, it is nearly lunch. Will you dine with me?"

"I would be delighted, Holmes," said I. "I can spare another hour to enjoy one of Mrs. Hudson's meals."

"That is well, because I believe that Mrs. Hudson has prepared roast beef, which I know to be a favorite of yours."

"Another deduction, Holmes?" I asked, laughing.

"The fact that roast beef is a favorite of yours is known to me from our long association, but as to the meal itself, that is a deduction of the nose, old friend," said he. "I detect the odor of the meal wafting up from below."

"Outstanding, Holmes," I said with a smile.

"Elementary," he replied with a grin playing about his lips. "And as I hear the familiar tread of Mrs. Hudson's step upon the stairs, let us remove ourselves to the table. We must keep our strength up. Perhaps the afternoon will bring a new case."

I agreed, and followed the great detective to the dining room. I hoped in my heart that Holmes would be correct, and that a new case was just beyond the horizon.

The End

SPECIAL NOTE

If you've read and enjoyed The Sherlock Holmes Uncovered Tales, please add a review at the site on which you purchased your copy. Reviews provide a valuable guide for those attempting to find books they might enjoy.

Thank you,

Steven Ehrman

35451384R00074

Made in the USA
Middletown, DE
04 October 2016